For Xina
Love
Ann McG

ARROW BOOK OF

POETRY

Selected by ANN McGOVERN

Illustrated by GRISHA DOTZENKO

SCHOLASTIC BOOK SERVICES

NEW YORK · TORONTO · LONDON · AUCKLAND · SYDNEY · TOKYO

ISBN: 0-590-05424-4

Copyright © 1965 by Scholastic Magazines, Inc. This edition is published by Scholastic Book Services, a division of Scholastic Magazines, Inc.

23 22 21 20 19 18 17 16 15 14   2 3 4 5 6/8
Printed in the U.S.A.   11

ACKNOWLEDGMENTS

For reprint permission, grateful acknowledgment is made to:

Atheneum Publishers for "Which Washington?" "Where Is a Poem?" "Summer Rain" from *There Is No Rhyme for Silver*, ©1962 by Eve Merriam; " 'I' Says the Poem" from *It Doesn't Always Have to Rhyme*, ©1964 by Eve Merriam.

Augsburg Publishing House for "Cloud Horses" from *God's Wonderful World* by John Travers Moore, ©1964 by Augsburg Publishing House.

Rowena Bennett for "Color" and "Springtime in the Park" by Rowena Bennett.

Arthur S. Bourinot for excerpt from "Paul Bunyan" from *This Green Earth* by Arthur S. Bourinot.

Brandt & Brandt for "Nancy Hanks" by Rosemary Carr Benét and "Clipper Ships and Captains" by Stephen Vincent Benét from *A Book of Americans* by Rosemary and Stephen Vincent Benét, published by Holt, Rinehart and Winston, Inc. Copyright 1933 by Rosemary and Stephen Vincent Benét. Copyright renewed 1961 by Rosemary Carr Benét.

Chatto and Windus Ltd. for Canadian market rights to "Lone Dog" from *Songs to Save a Soul* by Irene Rutherford McLeod.

Thomas Y. Crowell Co. for "At Nighttime," "Weather Is Full of the Nicest Sounds," and "I Like It When It's Mizzly" from *I Like Weather* by Aileen Fisher, copyright ©1963 by Aileen Fisher.

Dodd, Mead & Co., Inc. for "I Meant to Do My Work Today" from *The Lonely Dancer* by Richard Le Gallienne. Copyright 1913 by Dodd, Mead & Co. Copyright renewed.

Contents

Where Is a Poem?

Where is a poem?
As far away
As a rainbow span,
Ancient Cathay,
Or Afghanistan;

Or it can be near
As where you stand
This very day
On Main Street here
With a poem
In your hand.

—EVE MERRIAM

"Here, in the middle, am I"

Wishes and
Feelings

Open Range

Prairie goes to the mountain,
   Mountain goes to the sky.
The sky sweeps across to the distant hills
And here, in the middle,
   Am I.

Hills crowd down to the river,
   River runs by the tree.
Tree throws its shadow on sunburnt grass
And here, in the shadow,
   Is me.

Shadows creep up the mountain,
   Mountain goes black on the sky,
The sky bursts out with a million stars
And here, by the campfire,
   Am I.

—KATHRYN AND BYRON JACKSON

Travel

The railroad track is miles away,
   And the day is loud with voices speaking,
Yet there isn't a train goes by all day
   But I hear its whistle shrieking.

All night there isn't a train goes by,
   Though the night is still for sleep and dreaming,
But I see its cinders red on the sky,
   and hear its engine steaming.

My heart is warm with the friends I make,
   And better friends I'll not be knowing,
Yet there isn't a train I wouldn't take,
   No matter where it's going.

—EDNA ST. VINCENT MILLAY

Whispers

Whispers
    tickle through your ea
    telling things you like to hea

Whispers
    are as soft as skin
    letting little words curl in.

Whispers
    come so they can blow
    secrets others never know.

— Myra Cohn Livingston

Afternoon on a Hill

I will be the gladdest thing
   Under the sun!
I will touch a hundred flowers
   And not pick one.

I will look at cliffs and clouds
   With quiet eyes,
Watch the wind bow down the grass,
   And the grass rise.

And when lights begin to show
   Up from the town,
I will mark which must be mine,
   And then start down!

           —EDNA ST. VINCENT MILLAY

I Meant to Do My Work Today

I meant to do my work today
But a brown bird sang in the apple-tree,
And a butterfly flitted across the field,
And all the leaves were calling me.

And the wind went sighing over the land,
Tossing the grasses to and fro,
And a rainbow held out its shining hand—
So what could I do but laugh and go?

— RICHARD LE GALLIENNE

I Woke Up This Morning

I woke up this morning
At quarter past seven.
I kicked up the covers
And stuck out my toe.
And ever since then
(That's a quarter past seven)
They haven't said anything
Other than "no."

They haven't said anything
Other than "Please, dear,
Don't do what you're doing,"
Or "Lower your voice."
Whatever I've done
And however I've chosen,
I've done the wrong thing
And I've made the wrong choice.

I didn't wash well
And I didn't say thank you.
I didn't shake hands
And I didn't say please.
I didn't say sorry
When, passing the candy,
I banged the box into
Miss Witelson's knees.
I didn't say sorry.
I didn't stand straighter.
I didn't speak louder
When asked what I'd said.
Well, I said
That tomorrow
At quarter past seven,
They can
come in and get me
I'M STAYING IN BED.

—Karla Kuskin

My Hole

I ran outdoors to dig a hole.
I dug it. It is deep.
I need this hole for keeping all
The treasures I must keep.

Like mushrooms.
Or some dried-up worms.
An acorn; peach or cherry pit.
When nobody's around I hide
Whatever I collect in it.

But, little creatures, if you're cold
When snow and winter blizzards come
Then gopher, chipmunk, mouse or mole—
Just make my hole your home.

—DOROTHY ALDIS

My Valentine

I will make you brooches and toys for your delight
Of bird song at morning and starshine at night.
I will make a palace fit for you and me,
    Of green days in forests
    And blue days at sea.

— ROBERT LOUIS STEVENSON

People Buy a Lot of Things

People buy a lot of things —
Carts and balls and nails and rings,
But I would buy a bird that sings.

I would buy a bird that sings and let it sing for me,
And let it sing of flying things and mating in a tree,
And then I'd open wide the cage, and set the singer free.

— ANNETTE WYNNE

This Is My Rock

This is my rock,
And here I run
To steal the secret of the sun;

This is my rock,
And here come I
Before the night has swept the sky;

This is my rock,
This is the place
I meet the evening face to face.

— DAVID McCORD

Sea Fever

I must go down to the seas again, to the lonely sea and
   the sky,
And all I ask is a tall ship and a star to steer her by,
And the wheel's kick and the wind's song and the white
   sail's shaking,
And a gray mist on the sea's face, and a gray dawn breaking.

I must go down to the seas again, for the call of the
   running tide
Is a wild call and a clear call that may not be denied;
And all I ask is a windy day with the white clouds flying,
And the flung spray and the blown spume, and the sea
   gulls crying.

I must go down to the seas again, to the vagrant gypsy life,
To the gull's way and the whale's way where the wind's
   like a whetted knife;
And all I ask is a merry yarn from a laughing fellow-rover,
And quiet sleep and a sweet dream when the long trick's over.

                          — JOHN MASEFIELD

The Dream Keeper

I loved my friend.
He went away from me.
There's nothing more to say.
The poem ends,
Soft as it began —
I loved my friend.

— Langston Hughes

Primer Lesson

Look out how you use proud words.
When you let proud words go, it is not easy to call them back.
They wear long boots, hard boots; they walk off proud; they
    can't hear you calling—
Look out how you use proud words.

— Carl Sandburg

Block City

What are you able to build with your blocks?
Castles and palaces, temples and docks.
Rain may keep raining, and others go roam,
But I can be happy and building at home.

Let the sofa be mountains, the carpet be sea,
There I'll establish a city for me:
A kirk and a mill and a palace beside,
And a harbor as well where my vessels may ride.

Great is the palace with pillar and wall,
A sort of a tower on the top of it all,
And steps coming down in an orderly way
To where my toy vessels lie safe in the bay.

This one is sailing and that one is moored:
Hark to the song of the sailors on board!
And see on the steps of my palace, the kings
Coming and going with presents and things!

Now I have done with it, down let it go!
All in a moment the town is laid low.
Block upon block lying scattered and free,
What is there left of my town by the sea?

Yet as I saw it, I see it again,
The kirk and the palace, the ships and the men,
And as long as I live, and where'er I may be,
I'll always remember my town by the sea.

ROBERT LOUIS STEVENSON

Sunset Blues

Seagulls' crying
on the edge of town
over the harbor
when the sun goes down

makes the loneliest
kind of cry,
makes me ache
that the day's gone by,
stings my throat
and itches my nose.
Guess they think when the old sun goes

that it falls in the sea
like a ripe beach plum,
that tomorrow is over
before it can come.

Guess they think
every sunset sky
is the world's last day
and it makes them cry.

Well, I know better.
The sun won't drown.
But when seagulls rise
on the edge of town

and call through the harbor
Bad news! Bad news!
I always get
those sunset blues.

—MAXINE W. KUMIN

Chanson Innocente

II

little tree
little silent Christmas tree
you are so little
you are more like a flower

who found you in the green forest
and were you sorry to come away?
see   i will comfort you
because you smell so sweetly

i will kiss your cool bark
and hug you safe and tight
just as your mother would,
only don't be afraid

look   the spangles
that sleep all the year in a dark box
dreaming of being taken out and allowed to shine,
the balls the chains red and gold the fluffy threads,

put up your little arms
and i'll give them all to you to hold
every finger shall have its ring
and there won't be a single place dark or unhappy

then when you're quite dressed
you'll stand in the window for everyone to see
and how they'll stare!
oh but you'll be very proud

and my little sister and i will take hands
and looking up at our beautiful tree
we'll dance and sing
"Noel Noel"

— E. E. CUMMINGS

Sea Shell

Sea Shell, Sea Shell,
Sing me a song, O please!
A song of ships, and sailor men,
And parrots, and tropical trees,

Of islands lost in the Spanish Main
Which no man ever may find again,
Of fishes and corals under the waves,
Of sea-horses stabled in great green caves.

Sea Shell, Sea Shell,
Sing of the things you know so well.

— AMY LOWELL

If All the Seas Were One Sea

If all the seas were one sea,
What a *great* sea that would be!
And if all the trees were one tree,
What a *great* tree that would be!
And if all the axes were one axe,
What a *great* axe that would be!
And if all the men were one man,
What a *great* man he would be!
And if the *great* man took the *great* axe,
And cut down the *great* tree,
And let it fall into the *great* sea,
What a splish splash *that* would be!

—Anonymous

"Who knows when the tiger passes?"

Creatures
Large

Color

Who knows when the tiger passes
through the stripes of jungle grasses
In his coat so subtly made
Half of sun and half of shade —
Who knows when the tiger passes?

Who can find a leopard sleeping
On the bough, beneath the creeping
Vine, his softly spotted
Fur amid the dotted
Shadow? Who believes
It's more than sun and leaves
When he sees a leopard sleeping?

Who can see a bear that goes
Riding on the Arctic floes?
When the long day glistens bright
Who can see white framed in white?
Seal and salmon, O take care
Lest upon you, unaware,
Come the snowstorm of a bear.

— Rowena Bennett

Catalog

Cats sleep fat and walk thin.
Cats, when they sleep, slump;
When they wake, pull in —
And where the plump's been
There's skin.
Cats walk thin.

Cats wait in a lump,
Jump in a streak.
Cats, when they jump, are sleek
As a grape slipping its skin —
They have technique.
Oh, cats don't creak.
They sneak.

Cats sleep fat.
They spread comfort beneath them
Like a good mat,
As if they picked the place
And then sat.
You walk around one
As if he were the City Hall
After that.

If male,
A cat is apt to sing on a major scale;
This concert is for everybody, this
Is wholesale.
For a baton, he wields a tail.
(He is also found,
When happy, to resound
With an enclosed and private sound.)

A cat condenses.
He pulls in his tail to go under bridges,
And himself to go under fences.
Cats fit
In any size box or kit;
And if a large pumpkin grew under one,
He could arch over it.

When everyone else is just ready to go out,
The cat is just ready to come in.
He's not where he's been.
Cats sleep fat and walk thin.

— ROSALIE MOORE

Cat

Cat!
Scat!
After her, after her,
Sleeky flatterer,
Spitfire chatterer,
Scatter her, scatter her
Off her mat!
Wuff!
Wuff!
Treat her rough!
Git her, git her,
Whiskery spitter!
Catch her, catch her,
Green-eyed scratcher!
Slathery
Slithery
Hisser,
Don't miss her!
Run till you're dithery,
Hithery
Thithery

Pftts! pftts!
How she spits!
Spitch! Spatch!
Can't she scratch!
Scritching the bark
Of the sycamore-tree,
She's reached her ark
And's hissing at me
Pftts's pftts!
Wuff! wuff!
Scat,
Cat!
That's
That!

— ELEANOR FARJEON

The Cat Heard the Cat-Bird

One day, a fine day, a high-flying-sky day,
A cat-bird, a fat bird, a fine fat cat-bird
Was sitting and singing on a stump by the highway.
Just sitting. And singing. Just that. But a cat heard.
A thin cat, a grin-cat, a long thin grin-cat
Came creeping the sly way by the highway to the stump.
"O cat-bird, the cat heard! O cat-bird scat!
The grin-cat is creeping! He's going to jump!"

— One day, a fine day, a high-flying-sky day,
A fat cat, yes, that cat we met as a thin cat
Was napping, cat-napping on a stump by the highway.
And even in his sleep you could see he was a grin-cat.
Why was he grinning? — He must have had a dream.
What made him fat? — A pan full of cream.
What about the cat-bird? — What bird, dear?
I don't see any cat-bird here.

— JOHN CIARDI

The Hairy Dog

My dog's so furry I've not seen
His face for years and years;
His eyes are buried out of sight,
I only guess his ears.

When people ask me for his breed,
I do not know or care;
He has the beauty of them all
Hidden beneath his hair.

— HERBERT ASQUITH

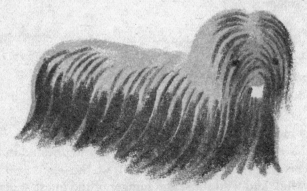

Lone Dog

I'm a lean dog, a keen dog, a wild dog, and lone;
I'm a rough dog, a tough dog, hunting on my own!
I'm a bad dog, a mad dog, teasing silly sheep;
I love to sit and bay the moon, to keep fat souls
    from sleep.

I'll never be a lap dog, licking dirty feet,
A sleek dog, a meek dog, cringing for my meat,
Not for me the fireside, the well-filled plate,
But shut door, and sharp stone, and cuff and kick and hate.

Not for me the other dogs, running by my side,
Some have run a short while, but none of them would bide.
O mine is still the one trail, the hard trail, the best
Wide wind, and wild stars, and hunger of the quest!

— IRENE RUTHERFORD McLEOD

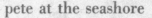

pete at the seashore

i ran along the yellow sand
and made the sea gulls fly
i chased them down the waters edge
i chased them up the sky

i ran so hard i ran so fast
i left the spray behind
i chased the flying flecks of foam
and i outran the wind

an airplane sailing overhead
climbed when it heard me bark
i yelped and leapt right at the sun
until the sky grew dark

some little children on the beach
threw sticks and ran with me
o master let us go again
and play beside the see
                    pete the pup

— DON MARQUIS

Foal

Come trotting up
Beside your mother,
Little skinny.

Lay your neck across
Her back, and whinny,
Little foal.
You think you're a horse
Because you can trot —
But you're not.

Your eyes are so wild,
And each leg is as tall
As a pole;

And you're only a skittish
Child, after all,
Little foal.

— MARY BRITTON MILLER

The Old Horse in the City

The moon's a peck of corn. It lies
Heaped up for me to eat.
I wish that I might climb the path
And taste that supper sweet.

Men feed me straw and scanty grain
And beat me till I'm sore.
Some day I'll break the halter-rope
And smash the stable-door,

Run down the street and mount the hill
Just as the corn appears.
I've seen it rise at certain times
For years and years and years.

—VACHEL LINDSAY

The Pasture

I'm going out to clean the pasture spring;
I'll only stop to rake the leaves away
(And wait to watch the water clear, I may):
I sha'n't be gone long.— You come too.

I'm going out to fetch the little calf
That's standing by the mother. It's so young
It totters when she licks it with her tongue.
I sha'n't be gone long.— You come too.

— ROBERT FROST

The Fox Rhyme

Aunt was on the garden seat
    Enjoying a wee nap and
Along came a fox! teeth
    Closed with a snap and
He's running to the woods with her
    A-dangle and a-flap and—
Run, uncle run
    And see what has happened.

—IAN SERRAILLIER

Cows

Half the time they munched the grass, and all the
   time they lay
Down in the water-meadows, the lazy month of May,
   A-chewing,
   A-mooing,
     To pass the hours away.

"Nice weather," said the brown cow.
   "Ah," said the white.
"Grass is very tasty."
   "Grass is all right."

Half the time they munched the grass, and all the
   time they lay
Down in the water-meadows, the lazy month of May,
   A-chewing,
   A-mooing,
      To pass the hours away.

"Rain coming," said the brown cow.
   "Ah," said the white.
"Flies is very tiresome."
   "Flies bite."

Half the time they munched the grass, and all the
   time they lay
Down in the water-meadows, the lazy month of May,
   A-chewing,
   A-mooing,
      To pass the hours away.

"Time to go," said the brown cow.
   "Ah," said the white.
"Nice chat." "Very pleasant."
   "Night." "Night."

Half the time they munched the grass, and all the
   time they lay
Down in the water-meadows, the lazy month of May,
   A-chewing,
   A-mooing,
      To pass the hours away.

—JAMES REEVES

"I heard a bird sing"

Creatures
Small

I Heard a Bird Sing

I heard a bird sing
   In the dark of December
A magical thing
   And sweet to remember.
"We are nearer to Spring
   Than we were in September,"
I heard the bird sing
   In the dark of December.

—OLIVER HERFORD

Sea Gull

The sea gull curves his wings,
the sea gull turns his eyes.
Get down into the water, fish!
(if you are wise.)

The sea gull slants his wings,
the sea gull turns his head.
Get deep into the water, fish!
(or you'll be dead.)

—ELIZABETH COATSWORTH

Regent's Park

What makes the ducks in the pond, I wonder, go
Suddenly under?

Down they go in the neatest way;
You'd be surprised at the time they stay;
You stand on the bank and you wait and stare,
Trying to think what they do down there;
And just as you're feeling anxious, then
Suddenly up they come again,
Ever so far from where you guessed,
Dry and tidy and self-possessed.

What is it makes the duck, I wonder, go
Suddenly under?

— ROSE FYLEMAN

Advice to a Bird, Species Unknown

Listen to me, you silly bird,
Has no one told you? Haven't you heard
That the winters here are long and cold?
Then harken, bird. You are being told.
Be on your way! Go south! Get going!
Any time now it may be snowing,
Sleet and hail and a mean wind blowing.

Winter is here. Didn't you know that?
And winter's a crusty old gray cat,
Ice on his whiskers, frost on his paws.
He'll gobble you up in his freezing jaws!
He'll snap you up in his arctic mouth!
I'm telling you, bird, be bright. Go south!

— Georgie Starbuck Galbraith

Snail

Snail upon the wall,
Have you got at all
Anything to tell
About your shell?

Only this, my child—
When the wind is wild,
Or when the sun is hot,
It's all I've got.

—JOHN DRINKWATER

Quick as a Wink

I tried to catch a grasshopper
Quick as a wink he spit at me
His juice was brown. It stained my shirt.
Leave me alone I must be free.

I stood and watched him longingly.
I would love to jump that high.
But anyone at all could see
He was glad he wasn't me.

—DOROTHY ALDIS

The Caterpillar

Brown and furry
Caterpillar in a hurry;
Take your walk
To the shady leaf or stalk.

May no toad spy you,
May the little birds pass by you;
Spin and die,
To live again a butterfly.

—CHRISTINA GEORGINA ROSSETTI

Goodbye

Hear a tiny orchestra
Fiddle the summer through.
Crickets fiddle with their wings.
Katydids do too.
They tell us first what Katy did,
Then what she didn't do.

But when it's chilly on the lawn,
Cold in fields of clover,
They fold their little instruments.
Goodbye.
The concert's over.

— DOROTHY ALDIS

The Snare

I hear a sudden cry of pain!
There is a rabbit in a snare;
Now I hear the cry again,
But I cannot tell from where.

But I cannot tell from where.
He is calling out for aid!
Crying on the frightened air,
Making everything afraid!

Making everything afraid!
Wrinkling up his little face!
As he cries again for aid;
— And I cannot find the place!

And I cannot find the place
Where his paw is in the snare!
Little One! Oh, Little One!
I am searching everywhere!

— JAMES STEPHENS

To a Squirrel at Kyle-Na-No

Come play with me;
Why should you run
Through the shaking tree
As though I'd a gun
To strike you dead?
When all I would do
Is to scratch your head
And let you go.

— W. B. YEATS

Where Is It?

He flips his tail
  And points his nose
And digs it up
  With frantic claws—
That nut he buried
  Long ago
When there wasn't
  Any snow.

He holds it tight
  Between his paws,
Cracks it with
  His little jaws,
And eats it up,
  Then off he goes...

But how is he sure a nut's still there?
And how can he guess exactly where?
Squirrel never needs to guess.
He knows.

— DOROTHY ALDIS

"I like it when it's mizzly"

Weather Moods

I Like It When It's Mizzly

I like it when it's mizzly
and just a little drizzly
so everything looks far away
and make-believe and frizzly.

I like it when it's foggy
and sounding very froggy.
I even like it when it rains
on streets and weepy windowpanes
and catkins in the poplar tree
and *me*.

— AILEEN FISHER

57

Weather Is Full of the Nicest Sounds

Weather is full
of the nicest sounds:
it sings
and rustles
and pings
and pounds
and hums
and tinkles
and strums
and twangs
and whishes
and sprinkles
and splishes
and bangs
and mumbles
and grumbles
and rumbles
and flashes
and CRASHES.
I wonder
if thunder
frightens a bee,
a mouse in her house,
a bird in a tree,
a bear
or a hare
or a fish in the sea?
·Not *me!*

— AILEEN FISHER

Fog

The fog comes
on little cat feet.

It sits looking
over harbor and city
on silent haunches
and then, moves on.

—CARL SANDBURG

April Rain Song

Let the rain kiss you.
Let the rain beat upon your head with silver
   liquid drops.
Let the rain sing you a lullaby.

The rain makes still pools on the sidewalk.
The rain makes running pools in the gutter.
The rain plays a little sleep-song on our roof at
   night—

And I love the rain.

—LANGSTON HUGHES

Summer Rain

A shower, a sprinkle,
A tangle, a tinkle,
Greensilver runs the rain.

Like salt on your nose,
Like stars on your toes,
Tingles the tangy rain.

A tickle, a trickle,
A million-dot freckle
Speckles the spotted rain.

Like a cinnamon
Geranium
Smells the rainingest rain!

—EVE MERRIAM

The Noise of Waters

All day I hear the noise of water
    Making moan,
Sad as the sea-bird is, when going
    Forth alone,
He hears the winds cry to the waters'
    Monotone.

The grey winds, the cold winds are blowing
    Where I go.
I hear the noise of many waters
    Far below.
All day, all night I hear them flowing
    To and fro.

                    — JAMES JOYCE

The Moon's the North Wind's Cooky
(What the Little Girl Said)

The Moon's the North Wind's cooky.
He bites it, day by day,
Until there's but a rim of scraps
That crumble all away.

The South Wind is a baker.
He kneads clouds in his den,
And bakes a crisp new moon *that ... greedy*
North ... Wind ... eats ... again!

                    — VACHEL LINDSAY

"From the top of a bridge

Town and City
Moment

The River Is a Piece of Sky

From the top of a bridge
The river below
Is a piece of sky—
  Until you throw
  A penny in
  Or a cockleshell
  Or a pebble or two
  Or a bicycle bell
  Or a cobblestone
  Or a fat man's cane—
And then you can see
It's a river again.
The difference you'll see
When you drop your penny:
The river has splashes,
The sky hasn't any.

— JOHN CIARDI

City

In the morning the city
Spreads its wings
Making a song
In stone that sings,

In the evening the city
Goes to bed
Hanging lights
About its head.

—LANGSTON HUGHES

Skyscrapers

Do skyscrapers ever grow tired
Of holding themselves up high?
Do they ever shiver on frosty nights
With their tops against the sky?
Do they feel lonely sometimes
Because they have grown so tall?
Do they ever wish they could lie right down
And never get up at all?

—RACHEL FIELD

Every Time I Climb a Tree

Every time I climb a tree
Every time I climb a tree
Every time I climb a tree
I scrape a leg
Or skin a knee
And every time I climb a tree
I find some ants
Or dodge a bee
And get the ants
All over me.

And every time I climb a tree
Where have you been?
They say to me
But don't they know that I am free
Every time I climb a tree?
I like it best
To spot a nest
That has an egg
Or maybe three.

And then I skin
The other leg
But every time I climb a tree
I see a lot of things to see
Swallows rooftops and TV
And all the fields and farms there be
Every time I climb a tree
Though climbing may be good for ants
It isn't awfully good for pants
But still it's pretty good for me
Every time I climb a tree.

— DAVID MCCORD

Railroad Reverie

The little boy stopped in the middle of the hayfield
And cocked his head and listened for the sound.
It was there, it was coming, it was growing, it was coming.
Far away, but growing nearer, growing nearer, growing
   nearer,
Coming closer, coming closer, coming closer all the while;
Rumble-rumble, rattle-rattle, clatter-clatter, clank-clank,
Chugger-chugger, chugger-chugger, and it reached the
   final mile.

The little boy, rooted in the middle of the hayfield,
Cupped his eyes to shade them from the sun,
And heard the far-off whistle and the far-off rumble
And the far-off rattle of the railroad tracks
As the heavy giant train roared on.
Catch-a-teacher, catch-a-teacher, patch-his-britches,
Patch-his-britches, catch-a-teacher-patch-his-britches,
Catch-a-teacher   Whoosh!

Chugger-chugger, chugger-chugger, smoke upon the
    hayfield,
Cinders in the boy's hair and soot upon his face;
Laughter in the boy's heart, joy in the boy's feet,
Laughter in the engineer's face.
Chuggerchugger growing fainter
Catchateacher patchisbritches
Catchateacherpatchisbritches
Chuggerchugger sssssssssss

And the little boy turns to other business of the day
As the heavy giant rumble rumbles out and fades away.

—E. R. YOUNG

The Pickety Fence

The pickety fence
The pickety fence
Give it a lick it's
The pickety fence
Give it a lick it's
A clickety fence
Give it a lick it's
A lickety fence
Give it a lick
Give it a lick
Give it a lick
With a rickety stick
Pickety
Pickety
Pickety
Pick

— DAVID McCORD

Potomac Town in February

The bridge says: Come across; try me; see how good I am.
The big rock in the river says: Look at me; learn how
  to stand up.
The white water says: I go on; around, under, over, I
  go on.
A kneeling, scraggly pine says: I am here yet; they
  nearly got me last year.
A sliver of moon slides by on a high wind calling: I know
  why; I'll see you tomorrow; I'll tell you everything
  tomorrow.

—Carl Sandburg

"The buffaloes are gone"

Long Ago

Buffalo Dusk

The buffaloes are gone.
And those who saw the buffaloes are gone.
Those who saw the buffaloes by thousands and how they
    pawed the prairie sod into dust with their hoofs,
        their great heads down pawing on in a great pageant
    of dusk,
Those who saw the buffaloes are gone.
And the buffaloes are gone.

—CARL SANDBURG

Indians

Margaret mentioned Indians
And I began to think about Indians —

Indians once living
Where now we are living —

And I thought how little I know
About Indians. Oh, I know

What I have heard. Not much,
When I think how much

I wonder about them,
when a mere mention of them,

Indians, starts me. I
Think of their wigwams. I

think of canoes. I think
Of quick arrows. I think

Of things Indian. And still
I think of their bright, still

Summers, when these hills
And meadows on these hills

Shone in the morning
Suns before this morning.

—JOHN FANDEL

Nancy Hanks

If Nancy Hanks
Came back as a ghost,
Seeking news
Of what she loved most,
She'd ask first
"Where's my son?
What's happened to Abe?
What's he done?

"Poor little Abe,
Left all alone
Except for Tom,
Who's a rolling stone;
He was only nine
The year I died.
I remember still
How hard he cried.

"Scraping along
In a little shack,
With hardly a shirt
To cover his back,
And a prairie wind
To blow him down,
Or pinching times
If he went to town.

"You wouldn't know
About my son?
Did he grow tall?
Did he have fun?
Did he learn to read?
Did he get to town?
Do you know his name?
Did he get on?"

— ROSEMARY AND
    STEPHEN VINCENT BENÉT

Which Washington?

There are many Washingtons:
Which one do you like best?
The rich man with his powdered wig
And silk brocaded vest?

The sportsman from Virginia
Riding with his hounds,
Sounding a silver trumpet
On the green resplendent grounds?

The President with his tricorne hat
And polished leather boots,
With scarlet capes and ruffled shirts
And fine brass-buttoned suits?

Or the patchwork man with ragged feet,
Freezing at Valley Forge,
Richer in courage than all of them —
Though all of them were George.

— Eve Merriam

Grandmother's Brook

Grandmother tells me about a brook
    She used to pass on her way to school;
A quick, brown brook with a rushing sound,
    And moss-green edges, thick and cool.
When she was the age that I am now
    She would cross over it, stone by stone.
I like to think how she must have looked
    Under the greenery, all alone.
Sometimes I ask her: "Is it there,
    That brook you played by — the same, today?"
And she says she hasn't a doubt it is —
    It's children who change and go away.

— RACHEL FIELD

Paul Bunyan

He came,
striding
over the mountain,
the moon slung on his back,
like a pack,
a great pine
stuck on his shoulder
swayed as he walked,
as he talked
to his blue ox
Babe;
a huge, looming shadow
of a man,
clad
in a mackinaw coat,

his logger's shirt
open at the throat
and the great mane of hair
matching,
meeting
the locks of night,
the smoke from his cauldron pipe
a cloud on the moon
and his laugh
rolled through the mountains
like thunder
on a summer night
while the lightning of his smile
split the heavens
asunder.

— ARTHUR S. BOURINOT

Clipper Ships and Captains

There was a time before our time,
It will not come again,
When the best ships still were wooden ships,
But the men were iron men.

From Stonington to Kennebunk
The Yankee hammers plied,
To build the clippers of the wave
That were New England's pride.

The "Flying Cloud," the "Northern Light,"
The "Sovereign of the Seas" —
There was salt music in the blood
that thought of names like these.

"Sea Witch," "Red Jacket," "Golden Age,"
And "Chariot of Fame" —
The whole world gaped to look at them
Before the steamship came.

Their cargoes were of tea and gold,
And their bows a cutting blade;
And, on the poop, the skippers walked,
Lords of the China trade;

The skippers with the little beards
And the New England drawl,
Who knew Hong Kong and Marblehead
And the Pole Star over all.

Stately as churches, swift as gulls,
They trod the oceans, then;
No man had seen such ships before
And none will see again.

— ROSEMARY AND STEPHEN VINCENT BENÉT

From Season to Season

Something Told the Wild Geese

Something told the wild geese
    It was time to go.
Though the fields lay golden
    Something whispered — "Snow."
Leaves were green and stirring,
    Berries, luster-glossed,
But beneath warm feathers
    Something cautioned — "Frost."

All the sagging orchards
    Steamed with amber spice,
But each wild breast stiffened
    At remembered ice.
Something told the wild geese
    It was time to fly —
Summer sun was on their wings,
Winter in their cry.

             — RACHEL FIELD

At Nighttime

At nighttime
when it's light time,
and the snow turns blue,
and maple trees are empty
as the moon shows through,
and every star is shiny
as a silver spike,
I wonder
what the Weather
up in space
is like.

I wonder...
is there skating
on the far-off stars?
And snowy hills
for sliding
on a planet such as Mars?

I wonder how the mountains
of the moon must be
for skiers who are learning
how to ski... like me.

Some day
I'll take a rocket
(raisins in my pocket),
and zip away with Skipper
to the moon... and *see*.

— AILEEN FISHER

Stopping by Woods on a Snowy Evening

Whose woods these are I think I know.
His house is in the village though;
He will not see me stopping here
To watch his woods fill up with snow.

My little horse must think it queer
To stop without a farmhouse near
Between the woods and frozen lake
The darkest evening of the year.

He gives his harness bells a shake
To ask if there is some mistake.
The only other sound's the sweep
Of easy wind and downy flake.

The woods are lovely, dark and deep,
But I have promises to keep,
And miles to go before I sleep,
And miles to go before I sleep.

— ROBERT FROST

Spring Grass

Spring grass, there is a dance to be danced for you.
Come up, spring grass, if only for young feet.
Come up, spring grass, young feet ask you.

Smell of the young spring grass,
You're a mascot riding on the wind horses.
You came to my nose and spiffed me. This is your lucky year.

Young spring grass just after the winter,
Shoots of the big green whisper of the year,
Come up, if only for young feet.
Come up, young feet ask you.

— CARL SANDBURG

Springtime in the Park

I heard the springtime coming
   Across the winter snow.
I heard it in an icy brook
   That just began to flow.
I heard it in a running wind
   That pushed a cloud along.
And in some little hiding thing
   That made a chirping song.

— ROWENA BENNETT

Chanson Innocente

I

in Just-
spring   when the world is mud-
luscious the little
lame balloonman

whistles   far   and wee

and eddieandbill come
running from marbles and
piracies and it's
spring

when the world is puddle-wonderful

the queer
old balloonman whistles
far   and   wee
and bettyandisbel come dancing

from hop-scotch and jump-rope and

it's
spring
and
   the

      goat-footed

balloonMan   whistles
far
and
wee

— E. E. CUMMINGS

Cloud Horses

Sitting on a hilltop
Beneath a windy sky
And all about me the summer's hum:
Nothing like it on earth or on high —
The cloud horses, cloud horses, cloud
   horses come!

Storming down the twilight,
Straining at the dawn,
With streaming manes they carry on:
Silently galloping, vanishing some —
The cloud horses, cloud horses, cloud
   horses come!

— JOHN TRAVERS MOORE

Cricket Songs

Behind me the moon
brushes a shadow of pines
on the floor lightly.

— KIKAKU

Little bird flitting,
twittering, trying to fly . . .
my, aren't you busy!

— BASHO

Turning from watching
the moon, my comfortable old
shadow led me home.

— SHIKI

When my canary
flew away, that was the end
of spring in my house. .

— SHIKI

Leaf falling on leaf,
on mounds of leaves, rain splashing
in pools of rain . . .

— GYODAI

In spring the chirping
frogs sing like birds . . . in summer
they bark like old dogs.

— ONITSURA

Splinter

The voice of the last cricket
across the first frost
is one kind of good-by.
It is so thin a splinter of singing.

— CARL SANDBURG

Index of Titles and Authors